Puss in Boots

First published in 2005 by
Franklin Watts
96 Leonard Street
London
EC2A 4XD

Franklin Watts Australia
Level 17/207 Kent Street
Sydney
NSW 2000

Text © Anne Cassidy 2005
Illustration © Roger Fereday 2005

A CIP catalogue record for this book is available
from the British Library.

ISBN 0 7496 6155 0 (hbk)
ISBN 0 7496 6167 4 (pbk)

Series Editor: Jackie Hamley
Series Advisor: Dr Barrie Wade
Series Designer: Peter Scoulding

Printed in China

Puss in Boots

Retold by Anne Cassidy

Illustrated by Roger Fereday

W
FRANKLIN WATTS
LONDON•SYDNEY

The miller's son was very
poor. All he owned was
a talking cat called Puss.

Puss told the miller's son:
"Give me some boots
and a bag, and I'll make
you rich."

"I'll call you the Marquis of Carabas," said Puss. "Do everything I say and your dreams will come true!"

7

Puss told the miller's son to wait. Then he used his bag to catch a rabbit and he took it to the royal palace.

"This is a gift from the Marquis of Carabas," said Puss. The King and Princess were pleased.

9

Puss took other gifts to
the palace.

Each time, he said they
were from the Marquis
of Carabas.

One day, the King and
Princess came riding by.

Puss told his master jump
into the river. Then Puss
hid his clothes.

"Help! The Marquis of Carabas has been robbed! He's drowning!" shouted Puss.

The King's servants saved the miller's son and gave him some clothes. The Princess smiled. "Thank you for the gifts, Marquis."

The King and the Princess
offered to take their new
friend back to his castle.

"But I have no castle,"
whispered the miller's son.
Puss had a plan. "Follow
me!" he said and he ran off.

Nearby was a beautiful castle, owned by a terrible ogre. Puss spoke to the ogre's servants.

"Tell the King that the Marquis of Carabas is your master, or there'll be trouble!" he said.

"Who owns these woods and fields?" asked the King as he rode by.

"The Marquis of Carabas," came the reply from the ogre's servants.

Puss ran ahead to the castle. Then he went to find the ogre.

"Dear ogre, I have heard that you can turn into a lion!" said Puss.

The ogre was surprised to
see a talking cat, but he
turned into a lion and
roared at Puss.

"That's good," said Puss.
"But I bet you can't turn
into something small, like
a mouse!"

The ogre turned into a
tiny mouse ...

... and Puss ate him up!

Soon the King arrived.
"Who owns this beautiful
castle?" he asked.

"The Marquis of Carabas,"
replied Puss. The King and
Princess were delighted.

29

The Princess and the miller's son got married.

And Puss lived happily
ever after!

Leapfrog has been specially designed to fit the requirements of the National Literacy Strategy. It offers real books for beginning readers by top authors and illustrators.

There are 37 Leapfrog stories to choose from:

* hardback